# See Otto

# See Otto

### story and pictures by
### DAVID MILGRIM

Aladdin Paperbacks
New York  London  Toronto  Sydney

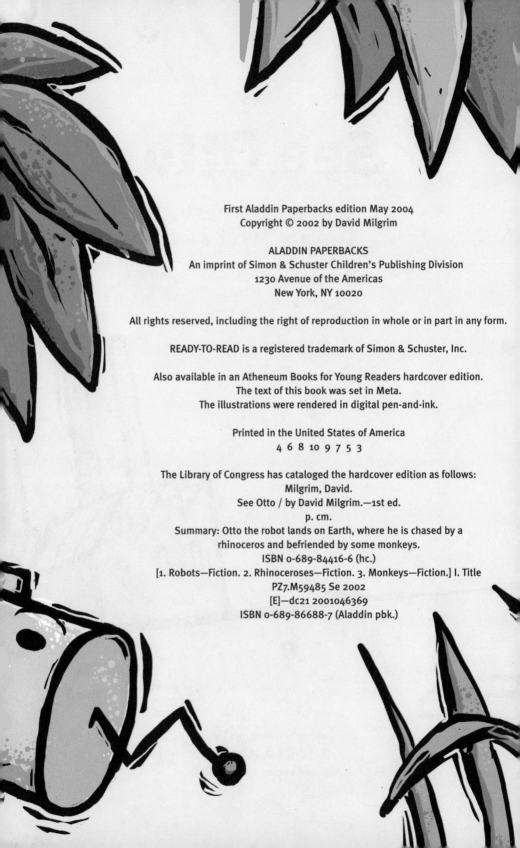

First Aladdin Paperbacks edition May 2004
Copyright © 2002 by David Milgrim

**ALADDIN PAPERBACKS**
An imprint of Simon & Schuster Children's Publishing Division
1230 Avenue of the Americas
New York, NY 10020

READY-TO-READ is a registered trademark of Simon & Schuster, Inc.

Also available in an Atheneum Books for Young Readers hardcover edition.
The text of this book was set in Meta.
The illustrations were rendered in digital pen-and-ink.

Printed in the United States of America
4  6  8  10  9  7  5  3

The Library of Congress has cataloged the hardcover edition as follows:
Milgrim, David.
See Otto / by David Milgrim.—1st ed.
p. cm.
Summary: Otto the robot lands on Earth, where he is chased by a
rhinoceros and befriended by some monkeys.
ISBN 0-689-84416-6 (hc.)
[1. Robots—Fiction. 2. Rhinoceroses—Fiction. 3. Monkeys—Fiction.] I. Title
PZ7.M59485 Se 2002
[E]—dc21  2001046369
ISBN 0-689-86688-7 (Aladdin pbk.)

For Kyra

See Otto.

See Otto go.

Go,
Otto,
go!

Go, go, go.

Look, Otto is out of gas.

# See Otto fall.

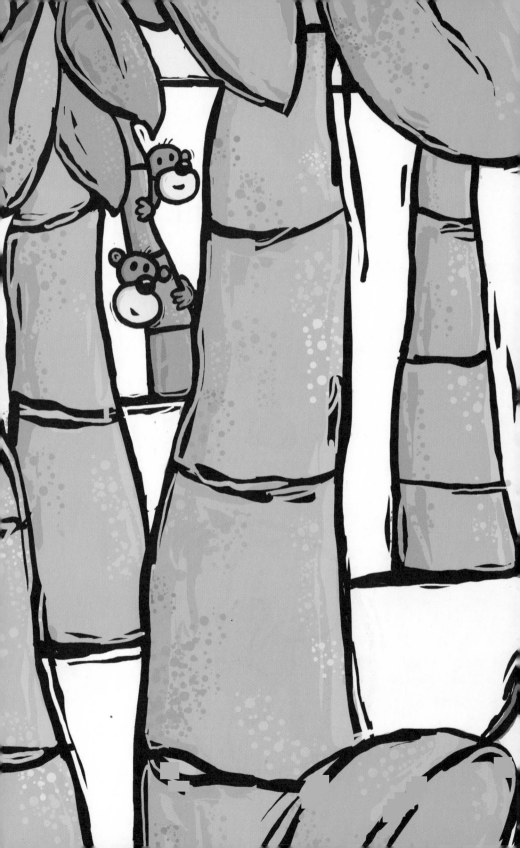

See Otto smile.

Smile, Otto, smile.

See
Otto
run.

See Otto fly.

Bye, Otto, bye.

# See Flip.
# See Flip paint.

See Flop.
See Flop sit.

Look, here comes Otto!

See paint fly.
Fly, paint, fly.

See everyone laugh.

Laugh, everyone, laugh.